BAD KITTY
Kitten Trouble

NICK BRUEL

ROARING BROOK PRESS
NEW YORK

For Robert
and all the dashing Daciws

Library of Congress Control Number 2018944870

ISBN: 978-1-250-18208-1

Our books may be purchased in bulk for promotional, educational, or business use.
Please contact your local bookseller or the Macmillan Corporate and Premium Sales
Department at (800) 221-7945 ext. 5442 or by e-mail at
MacmillanSpecialMarkets@macmillan.com.

First edition, 2018
Printed in the United States of America by LSC Communications,
Harrisonburg, Virginia

3 5 7 9 10 8 6 4 2

• CONTENTS •

•PROLOGUE•
EIGHT YEARS AGO

SNIFF
SNIFF
SNIFF

WAHHHH!

•CHAPTER ONE•
TODAY, MONDAY

Eight years later . . .

Kitty doesn't like that kid who delivers the newspapers.

Every day, the same thing—he bonks her on the head with the newspaper, and then he rides off on his bike saying . . .

Kitty doesn't like that kid's bike. Kitty doesn't like that kid's bell. Kitty really doesn't like that kid at all. So Kitty decides to do something about it.

17

OPERATION: "SMASH THE

① PLACE IRRESISTIBLE BAIT IN MIDDLE OF ROAD TO LURE OBNOXIOUS KID.

② HIDE IN TREE WITH BOWLING BALL.→

TREE

BAG OF ROCKS

BARBELLS

ASSORTMENT OF POTS AND PANS →

BASEBALL BAT →

HAM AND OCTOPUS PIZZA

(IN CASE I GET HUNGRY.)

NEWSPAPER KID"

WAIT FOR UNSUSPECTING
D ROTTEN KID TO ARRIVE.

POUNCE ON DOPEY
D LIKE A

~~EROSHUS~~
~~FERROSIUS~~
~~UROSIUS~~ SAVAGE ANIMAL,
ONG WITH MY MANY
NSTRUMENTS OF DESTRUCTION.

← ME

HEH-
HEH-
HEH!

) IGNORE PLEAS FOR
MERCY.

6) WATCH AWFUL KID CRY!

7) LAUGH IN NASTY
KID'S FACE.

8) FINISH PIZZA.

25

KLACKITA-WAKITA-
CRASH-BASH-SMASH-
CLANG-BANG-BONG-
LOKITA-BOKITA-ZONK-
SHLABLAMMO!

BOOM!

Kitty really, REALLY doesn't like that newspaper kid.

CHAPTER TWO

THE BIG PLAN

Thanks for bringing in the newspaper, Kitty. Is there anything more peaceful than spending a quiet Sunday morning reading the news? I don't think so.

Now let's see . . . news, news, news. Where is the news? It's got to be in here somewhere. Hmmm . . . Ah-ha! Here it is!

Oh, dear! This is terrible news!

According to the paper, the conflict in the neighborhood next to ours is growing worse and worse!

Do you know what a "conflict" is, Kitty? A conflict is like a terrible argument that has gotten out of hand.

Sometimes, people don't even know who or what started the argument. Sometimes, people don't even know what they're fighting about. They just keep fighting!

And now the fighting has gotten so bad in that neighborhood—even the cat shelters have been destroyed!

All of their cages and toys and litter boxes have been ruined! Plus, they can't go to the park or the playground or anywhere outside because it's so unsafe.

The kittens are all scared. They're hungry and have no where to go.

It really makes you think about how good we have it here in our own peaceful neighborhood.

Well, I think it's time for us to so do something. We might not be able to end this conflict, but I think we can still help.

There are oodles and oodles of KITTENS who have lost their homes. I think we should bring some of them HERE.

I like this idea! We'll take a few kittens into our home so they can feel safe and loved until the conflict is over and . . . and . . .

Okay, Kitty. You're giving me that "I'm-really-annoyed-with-you-and-everything-you-stand-for" face. What's the problem?

No, Kitty, the kittens are not secretly dogs in disguise. They're kittens.

OOK-OOK-OOK!

No, Kitty, they're not secretly gorillas in disguise either.

They're kittens.

BLUH-BLUH-SLURP!

No, Kitty, they're not secretly vampires who will drink our blood when we're asleep.

They're kittens.

No, Kitty, they're not secretly flesh-eating zombies who will eat our brains and transform us into flesh-eating zombies like them.

They're kittens.

No, Kitty, they're not secretly three-eyed, giant octopus space aliens who will lay eggs in our ears and eventually take over the planet.

They're kittens.

No, Kitty, they're not secretly sick biological experiments that have gone horribly out of control and will infect us with their spores until our faces melt.

They're kittens.

But I have to say, Kitty, your charades skills have really improved.

That's enough, Kitty! We have the opportunity to do something good here, and we're going to take it.

We're going to bring some sweet, innocent kittens into our home, and there's nothing you can do about it!

Uh . . . Kitty. Why are you giving me that "I'm-really-annoyed-with-you-but-now-I-have-a-diabolical-plan-from-which-I-will-receive-cruel-pleasure-from-the-misery-of-others" face?

Kitty? Kitty?

HEH-HEH-HEH!

Uh-oh.

Becaus
NO ON
gets alo
with cat
Not eve
other ca

UNCLE MURRAY'S
FUN FACTS

WHY DO CATS NOT GET ALONG WITH OTHER CATS?

Some cats actually DO get along very well with other cats. For instance, many kittens who grow up together become cats who live very peacefully with each other.

MINE!

What about cats who don't grow up with other cats?

Cats, by nature, are territorial, which means that they tend to be very possessive of their space, their belongings, and even their owners. In other words—cats don't like to share, especially with other cats.

What will happen if a new cat is brought into a home where there's already a cat?

The old cat is NOT going to share with the new cat. The old cat is not being selfish. In its mind, the old cat is being protective of all the things it believes it owns.

MINE!

What if the new cat wants to share?

If the old cat catches the new cat playing with one of its toys

MINE!

or eating from its food bowl or even getting pets from their owner, the result could be some angry hissing, spitting, chasing, and even fighting.

What should an owner do if the cats are fighting?

The worst thing you can do is ignore the problem. DON'T ignore the problem! Even though cats will usually run away from each other before getting caught up in a heated battle, it's still possible for them to get hurt.

If you sense that a fight is about to begin, maybe because you see one cat is stalking another, the best thing to do is to break them up by loudly clapping your hands or splashing a little water on the cats.

What if one cat is starting more fights than the other?

MINE!

Try not to play favorites. "Punishing" one cat more than the other they will only make them both feel resentful. That will make YOU a part of the problem.

43

CHAPTER THREE

NEW ARRIVALS

Hello there, Strange Kitty. I didn't know you were a kitten rescue worker. It's so nice of you to escort the kittens here from the other neighborhood. How's the conflict going, S.K.?

Not good.
Not good at all.
I was born in that neighborhood, and I barely recognize it anymore.

Seriously bad!

Everyone's still fighting! The whole place has gone crazy!

Just plain nutso!

Lots of yelling! Lots of screaming! Lots of stuff being destroyed!

It's complete bedlam! BEDLAM, I tells ya!

No one even seems to notice the kittens.

And that's the real tragedy.

But the good news is that the United Neighborhoods is meeting today to try to find a peaceful resolution.

48

* Look for a Glossary of this kitten's words translated into English at the end of this book.

51

KITTENS! KITTENS! It's okay! This is Puppy! He lives here, and he's very nice. I promise he won't hurt you!

LICKETY-SLURPITY-LICKETY-SLURPITY-LICKETY-SLURPITY-LICKETY-LICKETY-SLURP!

But you may want to think about taking a bath later.

There's someone else you need to meet, kittens. She's not quite as friendly as Puppy, but she does have a good side. It's not always obvious, but I promise you it's there.

I'm just not sure where she is. Kitty?! Kitty?! Where can she be?

KITTY!

You should be ashamed of yourself! That is a terrible way to treat our guests!

I demand that you apologize to them right NOW!

That is the worst apology I've ever seen.

Kitty, you have so much, and they have so little. It's time you learned how to share. For instance, look at this massive pile of toys you have. You don't even play with most of them anymore. Why don't you let the kittens play with them?

Kitty, that is terrible! The kitten only wanted to play with Mousey-mouse a little. You have to learn how to share. You have so much, and they have so little. For instance, you haven't even eaten most of your breakfast.

KITTY!

What is wrong with you?! The kitten only wanted a little to eat. You have to learn how to share. You have so much, and they have so little. For instance, last week I bought you a brand new cat tree. I haven't seen you climb on it even once.

65

KITTY!

Look at what you just did!
You destroyed your cat tree AND you scared the kittens. All this, just because you don't want to share.

Kitty, I know sharing is not easy for you. It's not always easy for ANYONE. But you have to remember that these kittens come from a place of terrible conflict. Most of what they own was destroyed. Plus, loud noises can be especially frightening to them.

Now get up and help me find these kittens so we can make them feel safe again.

Kitty, the kittens have been missing for hours and you still haven't lifted a claw to help me find them! I've looked everywhere. They're very good at hiding. Living in a neighborhood with so much conflict has taught them how to hide from danger very well.

Hooray! You're finally getting up off that couch. Does this mean that you're actually going to use your finely honed feline tracking skills to help me find those kittens!

Oh. I see.

71

You found them, Kitty! Good job!

But why did you have to scream at them? Now they've run off yet again.

That does it! You've forced my hand, Kitty. I'm calling in good ol' **Uncle Murray**. He's the nicest guy we know, and he's going to show you the proper way to treat our guests.

I'll be right over!

UNCLE MURRAY'S FUN FACTS

DO CATS EVER LIVE IN GROUPS?

Cats are typically independent animals, which means that they are quite comfortable living all by themselves.

Female cats living in a group

Do cats ever CHOOSE to live in a group?

Sometimes, in the wild, a group of cats will gather together and form a colony, also known as a "clowder." Usually, these clowders are all female cats who collectively take care of their kittens. Interestingly, no one cat will be in charge. Unlike with dog packs, no one cat is the "alpha" cat.

But it's important to note that each cat in the clowder will still hunt for food alone. And if food is scarce, then the cats will become competitive with each other to protect their food and their kittens.

| No Food | ➡ | Conflict! |

Lots of Food ➡ No Conflict

On the other hand, if food is plentiful, perhaps because a human is feeding the entire clowder, then the need to be territorial and protective is removed and the whole clowder lives in relative peace and harmony.

What if one of the kittens in the clowder is a male?

If a kitten is male, he'll live among the female cats until he matures and becomes an adult cat. Then he'll move out to be on his own.

Then what?

Male cats tend to live by themselves. They might live NEAR a female clowder, but they don't live among them, and they don't like to live with other male cats. This is because male cats can be VERY territorial. In fact, the territory of a male cat can be as much as ten times larger than that of a clowder of females.

As far as wild cats are concerned, it's the male cats that have a harder time sharing than the females.

SCRATCH
SCRATCH

Male cat living by himself.

CHAPTER FOUR

GOOD OL' UNCLE MURRAY

77

*As seen in *Bad Kitty: Puppy's Big Day.*

*As seen in *Bad Kitty Goes to the Vet.*

*As seen in *Bad Kitty: Camp Daze.*

*As seen in *Bad Kitty vs Uncle Murray.*

*As seen in *Bad Kitty Takes the Test.*

But Uncle Murray, try to be reasonable. These kittens didn't do any of those things to you. They're completely innocent.

I'm not willing to take that chance! I still can't look at a spatula without flinching. I can't make pancakes without hyperventilating!

Do you see this?! Kitty is the worst of them, and even SHE agrees with me!

Uncle Murray! I'm surprised at you! These are just tiny, helpless kittens. You can't possibly imagine that they caused all that damage in their neighborhood. Everything you just described—that's what they're trying to escape from!

Oh, Uncle Murray. Don't be like that. You're a guest here as well. You can stay as long as you'd like.

SIGH.
Uncle Murray really is a nice guy. But he can be very
touchy.

98

UNCLE MURRAY'S REALLY
IMPORTANT RULES FOR CATS
STAYING IN UNCLE MURRAY'S
~~HOSE~~ HOUSE

① Do not in any way scare, startle, frighten, terrify, or in general freak out Uncle Mur~~

② Do not in any way bite, chomp, nibble upon, scratch, claw, lacerate, or in general damage Uncle Murray or any of his stuff.

③ At no time shall a spatula come into contact with Uncle Murray's head or any other part of his body. He bruises easily.

④ The owner of this ~~hose~~ house recognizes that sometimes shedding is inevitable. However,

109

CLOMP
CLOMP
CLOMP

WHEW!

All I am saying is give peace a chance

UNCLE MURRAY'S FUN FACTS

CAN CATS BE TRAINED TO GET ALONG WITH EACH OTHER?

Short answer: Yes. Long answer: Even if two or more cats can't get along, will never share, and always seem to fight, it IS possible for them to live together in peace. But they can't do it without YOUR help.

MINE

What can an owner do?

Remember how cats in the wild got along better when when they had more food? The same is true for cats inside houses. The more resources of their own they have, the less there is to fight about.

MINE!

Cats are territorial inside their home, too. So if you want them to live together without conflict, then they need to have fewer reasons to fight. Each cat should have its own food bowl, and it might be important to keep those bowls far away from each other. The same is true for water dishes, litter boxes, and even YOU.

126

But what if there is only one owner?

If it's difficult or chaotic to play with your cats together, then play with them separately. Play with one cat in one room and the other cat in another room. Or find someone who can play with one cat while you play with the other. Over time, you might be able to play with both cats in the same room, but it might take a while.

How long?

Honestly, your cats may never really learn to share with each other and play with each other the way you'd like. But if you make sure they all have enough resources at their disposal, then you can reduce the conflict a lot.

You'll never be able to force your cats to be best friends, but you can help them learn how to live in peace together. They're just like people that way.

•CHAPTER SIX•

HOME AGAIN

Well, well, well . . . look who's back. Welcome home, Kitty. Uncle Murray called and told me how much you both regretted your behavior. Do you have anything you want to say to me and the kittens?

How nice. You brought flowers. Flowers yanked out of our garden. I suppose this is your way of apologizing.

Okay, Kitty. Come with me. You can give them the flowers, and then you'll see what the kittens were up to while you were out.

Wi-Fi router
Password: kittensrule

Mini fridges

Covered throughout with catnip-infused cashmere

Game system

130

Gravy fountain

Flat screen TV with 175 channels, incl. CNN (Cat News Network)

Kibble dispensers

Library

Cup holder

131

The kittens felt pretty bad about your cat tree breaking, so they built you a new one. That's what they were talking to each other about just before you left.

See, Kitty. You were so concerned about how you thought the kittens might damage your way of life that you never thought about how they might make your life better. You just had to give them a chance.

Is there something you want to say to the kittens?

PEACE!

134

You miss them already, don't you, Kitty?

Don't worry, Kitty. We can always go visit the kittens in their own neighborhood.

SCRATCH

It's good to expose ourselves to different cultures. Learning about how other cats and people live is a good way to keep the peace alive.

SCRITCHITY
SCRATCHITY
SCRITCHITY
SCRATCHITY

NAH!
You keep
it, cat. I'm
over it.

Besides, you gave me
this awesome new
cup holder. I'd call
that an even trade,
wouldn't you?

PURRRR

•GLOSSARY•

The following is a list that translates one of the kitten's dialogue from French to English in the order in which it appears.

Bonjour (bon-joor)—Hello

J'aime votre chapeau (jhem vo-tra sha-po)—I like your hat

Sacre bleu (sa-kra bluh)—Sacred blue (an uncommon expression of surprise)

Un monstre (uhn mon-stra)—A monster

Petite souris (pe-tee soo-ree)—Little mouse

Zut Alors (zoot a-lor)—Darn (another uncommon expression of surprise)

Oh, la vache (o la vash)—Holy cow (a slightly more common expression of surprise)

Belles fleurs (bell flurs)—Pretty flowers

Merci (maer-see)—Thank you

Mon Dieu (mon dee-u)—My God

Au revoir, Cher Kitty (o rev-wahr cher Kit-ee)—Goodbye, dear Kitty